Something BIGGER Than Me

JAMARE HARRIS

ISBN: Softcover   978-1-5434-6542-6
        Hardcover   978-1-5434-6543-3
        EBook   978-1-5434-6541-9

Print information available on the last page

Rev. date: 01/09/2018

To order additional copies of this book, contact:
Xlibris
1-888-795-4274
www.Xlibris.com
Orders@Xlibris.com

To Kevin, my dad, for all the times you helped me find the answers to my endless questions... But especially for the times you knew to let the answer find me.

- H.R Keene

To Claudine, my aunt. Thank you for nurturing my gift even before I realized that it was one.

-J. Harris

Every Saturday morning, my poppa and I walk to the diner down the street. I shovel pancakes down my throat while he drinks his coffee. He teases me, "Son, the pancakes aren't going anywhere. Slow down!" He must have never eaten these pancakes before!

This Saturday wouldn't be any different. Well, except for a very important question that I had to ask him. Poppa always knows every answer to every question. I just knew that today wouldn't be any different. Well, at least I thought that it wouldn't be. I flew down the stairs.

"Poppa! I'm ready!"

My dad was in the kitchen, talking to my mom. "All right, Zeke, but you do know—"

"I know, I know, Poppa," I said. "The pancakes aren't going anywhere."

He chuckled.

I skipped over to my mom and gave her a kiss. "Are you coming with us this Saturday?" I asked even though I already knew the answer.

"No, honey, just you and Poppa." She winked.

I must admit, I did like hanging out with my dad. He called it "boys' day out." And anytime I questioned him about Mom coming along, he said that she needed "mommy time"—whatever that meant. I tugged at my dad's shirt.

"Uh . . . Poppa, can we go now? Pleeaassee."

"I'll race you to the door!" He gave me a head start.

Poppa opened the door to the diner. "Mmmmmm." I took in a deep breath. I could almost taste the pancakes.

We sat down at the same table every Saturday. It was by a huge window, and we enjoyed looking out of it.

As we waited for our food, I figured that this was the perfect time to ask Poppa this very important question. I took a deep breath.

"Hey, Poppa."

He broke his gaze from the window.

"Yes, Zeke," he said.

"I've been thinking," I said slowly, "and . . . I was wondering . . ." I hesitated.

My dad looked at me through squinted eyes. "Spit it out, son."

"Why, why did God make the world?" The words managed to escape from my mouth.

Poppa sat back and took a deep breath. He looked at me and said words that I wasn't expecting. "I don't know, Zeke. Why do *you* think he did?"

My jaw dropped.

"Dads don't know everything, my boy."

"They don't?" I asked quizzically. I was shocked!

Poppa smiled and continued to drink his coffee.

As we walked through the park on the way home, I replayed those words in my head: "Dads don't know everything." Poppa always knew the answer to all my other questions.

It was then that I realized that it was up to me to find the answer to why God made the world, so that Poppa *would* know everything.

When we got home, I waved to my mom and darted up the stairs to my room. I remembered my dad asking me why I thought that God made the world. That was something that I hadn't thought about. I thought that there was just one right answer. I began to look in books for the answer, but no luck there. That night, I asked to watch *The Lion King*. No answer there either.

The next morning, I was awakened by the sun shining through my window. *Hmmmm,* I thought. I jumped out of bed and grabbed a notebook out of my desk. I quickly drew a picture.

I went downstairs and saw my mom and dad giving each other a hug. I ran over to join them. "Hey, Zeke," they said in unison. I looked up at their faces. *Hmmmm,* I thought again. I ran back up to my room to draw another picture. I decided that it was best to keep my notebook with me for the rest of the day.

"Zeke," I heard my mother's voice from the bottom of the stairs. I slid across the floor at the top of the stairs. "Would you like to go for a walk after breakfast?" she asked.

Perfect, I thought. "I'll be ready in five!" I couldn't hide the smile on my face.

After breakfast, we took a nice long walk to the beach. On the way, I saw so many things to draw in my notebook.

"Hey, what ya got there?" My dad peeked over my shoulder.

I closed it quickly. "Top secret, Poppa."

"Fair enough." He smiled and walked away.

As we continued to walk, we arrived at the beach. I saw children splashing in the wide-open ocean. In the distance was a pod of dolphins, and everyone stopped to watch them. I think that I was beginning to understand why God made the world.

That night at dinner, I was ready to share my top secret notebook. I cleared my throat. "Mom, Poppa." I reached for my notebook and pulled out picture after picture. The drawings filled the table. "This," I began, "this is why God made the world."

My first picture was of me waking up this morning. "God made the sun to wake us up in the morning. He made the ocean to keep us cool on hot days and as a home for animals that swim." I showed them the picture of children splashing at the beach and the pod of dolphins. "God made trees for us to climb and to give us yummy fruit, not to mention the shade that they provide to us on hot days."

My mom picked up one of my sketches.

"And this?" she asked, holding up one of my drawings.

"Oh!" I exclaimed. "God made dogs to be a guide for people who can't see."

"Wow!" my parents said in a low whisper, with smiles spread across their faces.

I picked up my last picture, which was of my mom and dad giving each other a hug that morning. My mom placed her hand over her chest, while my dad gave her a look that only dads give to moms. I knew she would love this one.

"God made people to love other people."

My mom reached out for a hug, and I ran to her embrace.

"Zeke," she said. "You have answered a question that people have wondered for years."

"For years, really?" I replied. "It wasn't that hard to figure out."

My mom and dad laughed.

"So, you do know why God made children?" my dad asked.

"Oh no, Poppa, not another question you don't know!"

He laughed and tackled me with tickles. We collapsed onto the floor.

"Zeke, my boy."

"Yes, Poppa."

"God made children to help adults remember what they have sometimes forgotten. Thank you, son."

"No, Poppa, thank God."

Made in the USA
Monee, IL
19 December 2019